Best in Show

by Tracey West

Illustrated by Vincent Deporter

SCHOLASTIC INC.

New York Toronto London Auckland Sydney
Mexico City New Delhi Hong Kong Buenos Aires

© 2003 Viacom International Inc. All Rights Reserved.
Nickelodeon, SpongeBob SquarePants and all related titles,
logos and characters are trademarks of Viacom International Inc.

No part of this publication may be reproduced in whole or in part,
or stored in a retrieval system, or transmitted in any form or by
any means, electronic, mechanical, photocopying, recording,
or otherwise, without written permission of the publisher.

Published by Scholastic Inc.,
90 Old Sherman Turnpike, Danbury, Connecticut 06816.

SCHOLASTIC and associated logos are trademarks
and/or registered trademarks of Scholastic Inc.

ISBN 0-439-56278-3

First Scholastic Printing, December 2003

Chapters

Chapter 1
Squidward's Challenge

It was another busy day at the Krusty Krab. Behind the counter, Squidward Tentacles sighed as another fish came through the door.

"Oh joy—a customer," Squidward said in a flat voice. "Can I help you?"

"I'd like to hang up this sign," the fish said, handing Squidward a flyer. "It's for the Bikini Bottom Pet Show."

With a bored look, Squidward read
the flyer.

When SpongeBob SquarePants heard the news, he stopped flipping Krabby Patties. "Pet show?" he asked. "Why, my Gary is the best pet in all of Bikini Bottom. I know he could win!"

"Ha!" Squidward snorted. "If you ask me, that slimy snail of yours is no prizewinner."

SpongeBob flinched. "You don't mean that," he said. "You're just jealous because you don't have a pet to enter in the contest."

"Oh, yeah, SpongeBob SmartyPants?" Squidward shot back. "Well, maybe I do have a pet. It's a wonderful pet—a pet that will easily beat Gary in the Bikini Bottom Pet Show!"

Now SpongeBob was angry. He ran out of the kitchen and waved his fist at Squidward. "We'll see about that. Nobody insults my Gary and gets away with it!" SpongeBob cried.

Chapter 2
Meow!

After work, SpongeBob
raced home.

IS your pet
THE BEST?
PROVE IT!
Enter the 1st ever
BIKINI BOTTOM
PET SHOW!

GARY

"Gary, I have great news!" he said. "I entered you in the Bikini Bottom Pet Show."

"Meow!" Gary cried, quickly pulling his head and tail into his shell.

"Don't be nervous, Gary," SpongeBob said. "You're the best pet in the whole wide world, and it's time everybody knew it!"

Gary slowly poked one eyestalk out of his shell.

"That's the spirit, Gary!" SpongeBob
cheered. "We're going to win this pet show,
no matter what it takes!"

The pet show was a week away, and SpongeBob couldn't wait. He spent the time with Gary, training long and hard.

He waxed Gary's shell.

He massaged Gary's eyeballs.

And he taught Gary new tricks.

Finally, the big day arrived.

SpongeBob and Squidward lined up with the other contestants. Squidward kept his pet under a blanket.

"I'm Fred Fishley," said the host. "Welcome to the Bikini Bottom Pet Show. Let's give a big hand for our show's sponsor, Barnacle Bites."

Squidward made a face. "I'd never feed that squishy slop to *my* pet," he said.

The contestants filed onto the stage. SpongeBob eyed the blanket in Squidward's hands. "What is your pet anyway?" SpongeBob asked. "I don't

even think you have a pet."

Squidward grinned. "Aha, but you're wrong!" he said. He lifted the blanket. "Behold Rocky, my pet rock!"

"Ba-ha-ha-ha-ha!" laughed SpongeBob. "A rock? What kind of a pet is that?"

But the judges seemed impressed. "How original!" they exclaimed.

That made SpongeBob nervous. "This is going to be a close race," he told Gary. "Don't let me down!"

Soon it was time for the first competition.
"It's swimsuit time," announced Fred
Fishley. "Let's see what fashionable pets
are wearing to the beach these days."

First it was Rocky's turn. The judges
loved Rocky's seashell bikini.

"So stylish!" they said.

Then SpongeBob pushed Gary onto the stage. Gary slithered along in a shimmering, faux fur-trimmed mermaid suit.

"Work it, Gary! Work it!" SpongeBob yelled.

"Ooooh! Aaaaah!" cried the judges.

"That was great," SpongeBob congratulated Gary. "But we still have to wow the judges in the talent contest."

Squidward and Rocky went first.

"Rocky is the most obedient pet around," Squidward bragged. "Sit, Rocky! Stay, Rocky! Play dead, Rocky!"

Rocky did a perfect job. He didn't move once.

The judges loved it.

"What a smart rock!" they shouted.

SpongeBob started to panic. "Oh no!" he said. "The judges love Rocky. You'll have to give it all you've got, Gary."

"Meow?" Gary replied nervously.

"Don't be silly," SpongeBob said. "You've got to do this so that we can beat Squidward—I mean, win this contest!"

Gary did his tricks. He slid across a tightrope. He juggled fire with his eyestalks. And he wrote love notes to the judges in slime.

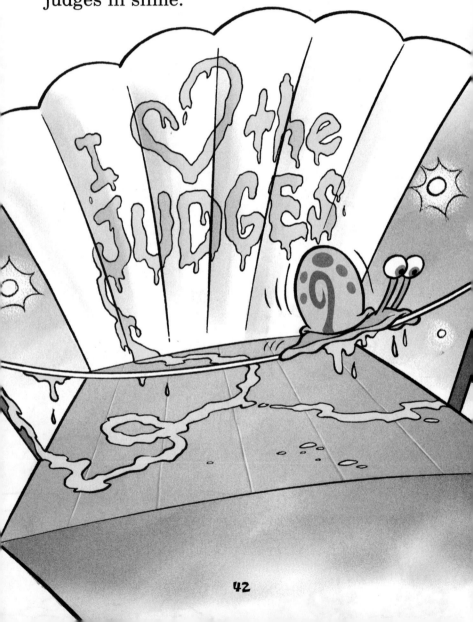

The judges clapped and cheered.

"Great job, Gary!" SpongeBob cried.

"There's no way we can lose now."

But the contest wasn't over yet.

"We've seen some amazing pets here today," Fred Fishley said. "But it all comes down to this final question."

"Okay, Rocky," Fred Fishley began, holding the microphone close to the rock. "What is the most important quality a pet can have?"

Rocky didn't make a sound.

Squidward smiled. "You know the saying," he said. "Silence is golden. Everyone loves a quiet pet."

"Brilliant!" said the judges.

Then it was Gary's turn.

"Gary, what would you say is the most important quality a pet can have?" Fred Fishley asked.

Gary looked at SpongeBob.

"Meow," he said.

"Gary says that a pet is also a friend," SpongeBob said. "And although friends do anything for each other, friends also respect each other's feelings."

"Wonderful!" said the judges.

"Meow," said Gary sadly. He slithered off the stage.

"Gary, where are you going?" SpongeBob asked. "Come back here, right now!"

Then SpongeBob stopped dead in his tracks. Suddenly it all started making sense. "Wait a minute . . . ," he said slowly. "I've been a terrible friend to you, Gary. You've done everything for me, and I haven't respected your feelings at ALL!"

SpongeBob burst into tears. "I'm so sorry, Gary," he said, hugging his pet. "This contest isn't about you. *I* pushed you into this. I was only thinking of me, me, ME!"

Gary snuggled up to SpongeBob. "Meow," Gary replied softly.

On stage, Fred Fishley was about to announce the winner. "And now for the moment you've all been waiting for," he said. "The best pet in all of Bikini Bottom is—"

"Just a minute!" SpongeBob interrupted, stepping onstage. "I'm sorry, but Gary has withdrawn from the contest," he declared. "Come on, Gary. Let's go home."

Fred Fishley looked confused for a moment. Then he spoke quietly with the judges.

When he returned, he announced, "Our first prize goes to—Rocky!"

Squidward waved proudly to the cheering crowd. "What can I say? The judges know a superior pet when they see one."

"Congratulations, Squidward and Rocky,"
Fred Fishley said. "And now for your prize:
Your picture will be on the label of
every can of Barnacle Bites."

"What kind of prize is that?" Squidward whined. "My perfect face on a can of that disgusting pet food?"

"Yes," said Fred Fishley, "on millions and millions of cans!"

"Noooooooooo!" wailed Squidward.

Later at home, SpongeBob prepared a special treat for Gary.

"Squidward might have won the prize," SpongeBob admitted. "But I've got the best pet—and the best friend—in all of Bikini Bottom!"

"Meow!" agreed Gary.